Just Around the Corner

JUST·AROUND·THE·CORNER

Leland B. Jacobs

ILLUSTRATED BY JOHN E. JOHNSON

Holt, Rinehart and Winston · New York · Chicago · San Francisco

For B. H. J. especially

Contents

Around the Corner

Just around the corner,
You just might meet
A happy young dinosaur
Walking in the street.

Just around the corner,
You just might see
An elfman riding
On a bumblebee.

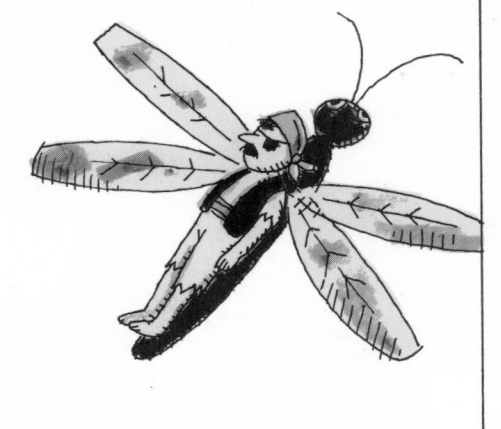

Just around the corner,
You just might note
A dancing bear
In an evening coat.

Just around the corner,
You just might spy
A pirate chained
To a dragonfly.

Just around the corner,
You just could sight
Something most unusual
If the times are right.

The High-Stepping Man

There once was a man
Who stepped so high
His knees touched the treetops,
His head touched the sky.

He stepped over mountains
And housetops and hills;
He stepped over flagpoles
And factories and mills.

This man of the high step
  Drew curious crowds
Which he never saw
  With his head in the clouds.

With his head in the clouds,
  How could he know
Just what was down
  Where his feet had to go?

The high-stepping man
  Is with us no more,
For he couldn't tell
  That he'd come to the shore.

How sad for the man
  With that high-stepping knee!
He stepped in the ocean
  And sank in the sea.

Going Somewhere

If you are going Somewhere . . .
  Where, oh where, is Somewhere?
Just around the corner,
  Just up the street,
Just a mile or two away
  Where two roads meet.
Just across the river,
  Or down by the pier,
Somewhere is anywhere
  That isn't right here.

Just

around the Corner to

SPRING

6

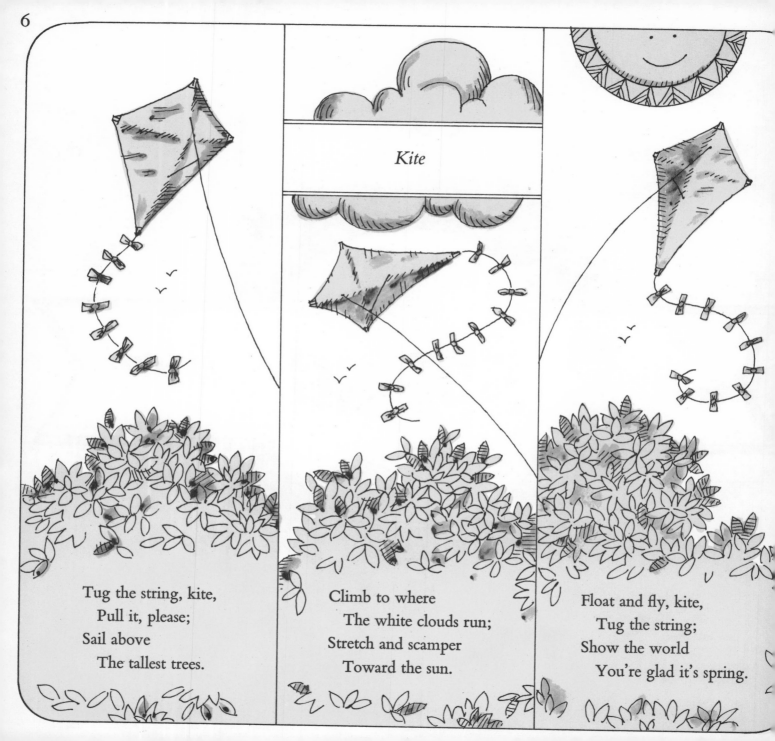

Kite

Tug the string, kite,
   Pull it, please;
Sail above
   The tallest trees.

Climb to where
   The white clouds run;
Stretch and scamper
   Toward the sun.

Float and fly, kite,
   Tug the string;
Show the world
   You're glad it's spring.

Solution

When I went out to play
  The day had just begun.
"Put on your coat," said the wind.
  "Take off your coat," said the sun.

Now who was in the right?
  And which advice was better?
I solved the problem for myself—
  I just put on my sweater.

8

For St. Patrick's Day

Fiddle tune,
Fiddle play,
Fiddle for St. Patrick's Day.
Tell of shamrock,
Fair to see,
Tell of Blarney's
Mystery.
Tell about
The fairy ring.
Fiddle sing,
Fiddle play,
Fiddle for St. Patrick's Day.

It's Spring!

Snapdragon, snap,
Toadstool, turn,
Pussy willow, purr,
Fireweed, burn,
Black-eyed Susan, wink,
Sweet William, sing,
Forget-me-not, remember
It's Spring! Spring! Spring!

Catnip, nip,
Dandelion, roar,
Dogwood, bark,
Pitcher plant, pour,
Bee balm, buzz,
Bluebell, ring,
Jack-in-the-pulpit
Preach today,
It's Spring! Spring! Spring!

Out in the Rain

Willie Duck and Wallie Duck
Went out in the rain to play,
Splashing in the puddles
In a very careless way.

Neither had a raincoat
And neither had a hat,
But their mother didn't worry
Or fret about that.

Willie Duck and Wallie Duck,
For almost an hour,
Without any rubbers on
Played in a shower.

Of course their mother saw them,
But she didn't scold.
She didn't even tell them
That they'd both catch cold.

Willie Duck and Wallie Duck
Were wet clear through.
And what about their mother?
She was out there too!

Dandelions have a magic
All their own.
I'm not sure if it happens
Night or noon;
It's done so soon.
They give their golden yellow
To the sun;
They give their feathery whiteness
To the moon.

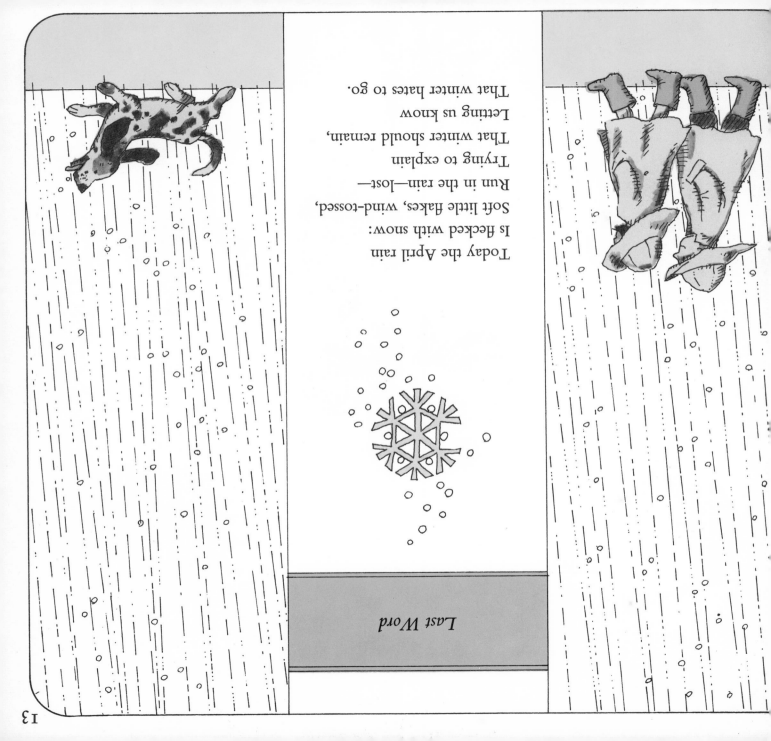

Last Word

Today the April rain
Is flecked with snow:
Soft little flakes, wind-tossed,
Run in the rain—lost—
Trying to explain
That winter should remain,
Letting us know
That winter hates to go.

Just About

I'm just about ready
　　To turn to a gnome.
I'm tired of staying
　　So close to home.

I'm just about ready
　　To turn to an elf.
I'm quite tired of being
　　Only myself.

I'm just about ready
　　To turn to a sprite,
But I'll be myself, home agai
　　Long before night.

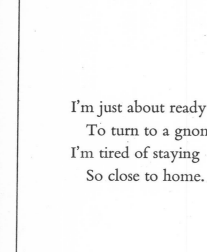

Just

around the Corner to

SUMMER

Shadows

The shadows of bushes
　Are much too small;
They hardly cover
　A child at all.

But the shadows of trees
　Are long and wide,
So that's the place
　Where I like to hide.

If I hide in the bushes
　Everyone sees
My arms and hands
　Or my legs and kne

But deep in the shado
　Of a tree,
Not even the sun
　Can discover me.

The Sun

Although it is gold,
　It isn't a locket;
Though shaped like a coin,
　It fits no pocket.

It hasn't a ladder,
　But it can climb.
It's much like a clock
　For telling the time.

It gives itself, free,
　To child and man,
But nobody touches it.
　Nobody can.

Shore

A shore is the place
   To play in the sand.
A shore is the place
   For digging a well.
A shore is the place
   To watch for a ship.
A shore is the place
   For finding a shell.
A shore is the place
   To lie in the sun
And watch the waves
   As they roll and run.
A shore is the place
   Where gulls fly free—
A shore is a wonderful
   Place to be.

Butterflies

Yellow butterflies
  And white
Use no map
  To guide their flight.

Up above
  The goldenrod,
Round about
  A milkweed pod,
They dart and flutter,
  Full of grace,
Then light and rest
  On Queen Anne's lace.

Yellow butterflies
  And white
Wing their way
  In chartless flight.

Night Song

When the sun has set
And night has come,
The insect chorus
Starts to hum.

And nothing else
Is there to hear,
But the insect voices
Soft and clear.

The insects hum
In sweet delight,
Singing their praises
Of the night.

Woodpecker

On the telephone pole
        I rap, rap, rap.
On the trunk of a tree
        I tap, tap, tap.
I peck, peck, peck,
        And I knock, knock, knock.
But don't turn the key
        And open the lock.
I never stop at a door to call,
For I'm not the visiting kind at all.
And if you should ask me in to play,
I'd simply have to fly away.

What the Brownie Kept

A brownie found a feather white.
　　He gave it to an elf.
He could have put it in his cap
　　And kept it for himself.

A brownie found a pebble bright.
　　He gave it to a gnome.
He could have kept it for himself
　　To brighten up his home.

A brownie found a milkweed pod.
　　He gave it to a sprite.
He could have kept it for a bed
　　To nestle in at night.

A brownie found a pumpkin seed—
　　He found it in a ditch.
Instead of keeping it himself,
　　He gave it to a witch.

The brownie found some special thing
　　Almost every day,
But all he kept was just the joy
　　Of giving things away.

Just

around the Corner to

FALL

Autumn's Return

The goldenrod wears yellow
curls,
The thistle's hair is white,
And clear and far the evening
star
Calls in the frosty night.

The leaves are showing buffs
and browns,
In red the sumacs burn,
And crickets muse the
headline news
Of autumn's swift return.

November Nights

November nights are
    purple nights—
    dusky purple deep—
And in the purple twilight,
    The summer flowers sleep.

November nights are
    purple nights.
    Now, when the shadows
      cling,
I dream of summer's heliotrope
    And lilac for the spring.

Quandary

Out in the grasses,
  Cleverly hid,
A voice keeps calling,
  "Katy did!"

"Katy did!"
  The voice will cry.
"Did what?" I ask,
  But there's no reply.

The voice repeats,
  In the weeds and clover,
"Katy did! Katy did!"
  Over and over.

So I'll never learn
  From the voice that's hid
Just what it was
  That Katy did.

Good Company

When other flowers
  Have gone away,
The goldenrod
  And asters stay.

The asters with
  Their purple blooms,
The goldenrod
  In yellow plumes,

Linger, though
  The others flee,
And keep
  October company.

Autumn Leaves

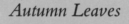

Green leaves,
Yellow leaves,
Red leaves, and brown,
Falling,
Falling,
Blanketing the town.

Oak leaves,
Maple leaves,
Apple leaves, and pear,
Falling,
Whispering,
"Autumn's in the air!"

Big leaves,
Little leaves,
Pointed leaves, and round,
Falling,
Nestling,
Carpeting the ground.

Autumn Bird Song

Over the housetops,
Over the trees,
Winging their way
In a stiff fall breeze,

A flock of birds
Is flying along
Southward, for winter,
Singing a song,

Singing a song
They all like to sing,
"We'll see you again
When it's spring, spring, spring."

On Halloween

Kitten, kitten,
  Don't go out.
Witches are flying
  All about.

Kitten, kitten,
  Stay inside
Or you'll be off
  On a broomstick ride.

It's Halloween,
  And witches roam,
So kitten, kitten,
  You must stay home.

At the Store

A lady cat once kept a store.
  Her store was just for kittens.
Now, what do you think the
    kittens bought?
  Calico for mittens,
Bright ribbons for around their necks,
  And catnip sweets for chewing,
And little cans of fish for lunch,
  And books to study mewing.

Fat Old Witch

The strangest sight
I've ever seen
Was a fat old witch
In a flying machine.

The witch flew high,
The witch flew low,
The witch flew fast,
The witch flew slow,
The witch flew up,
The witch flew down,
She circled all
Around the town.
Then, turning left
And turning right,
She disappeared
Into the night.

That fat old witch
In a flying machine
Is the strangest sight
I've ever seen.
Of course it happened
On Halloween.

Just around the Corner to

WiNTER

Snow Prints

Track of stag
   And track of doe
Print the pages
   Of the snow—
Print the snow
   With message clear,
Saying, stag and doe
   Were here.
But what their errand,
   Where they sped,
In the snow prints
   Can't be read.

What Do You Say?

What do you say
  To a bear that's waiting,
Just about ready
  For hibernating?

You don't say "Good evening,"
  It wouldn't seem right,
You'd not say "Good morning,"
  Or even "Good night."

I suppose you could say,
  "Good sleeping! Good rest!"
Or maybe "Good winter!"
  Would be the best.

Bear Coat

The polar bear, the
Polar bear—
He has a handsome
Coat to wear.

But, while it's thick and
Warm and white,
He has to wear it day and
Night.

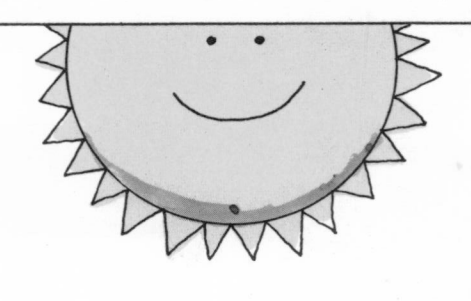

And when the summer
    Comes, poor brute,
He wears it for his swimming
    Suit.

Although his coat is thought
    So fine,
I'm very glad that it's
    Not mine.

Sneezing

Tell me, truly,
Tell me, please,
Tell me all
About a sneeze.

Is a sneeze
A cough grown small?
Or a wheeze
With a whistle call?

Tell me, truly,
Tell me, do,
Before I ask again . . .
Ah-choo!

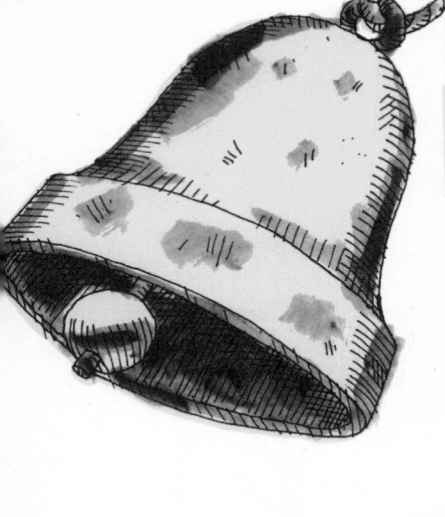

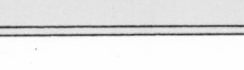
New Year Bells

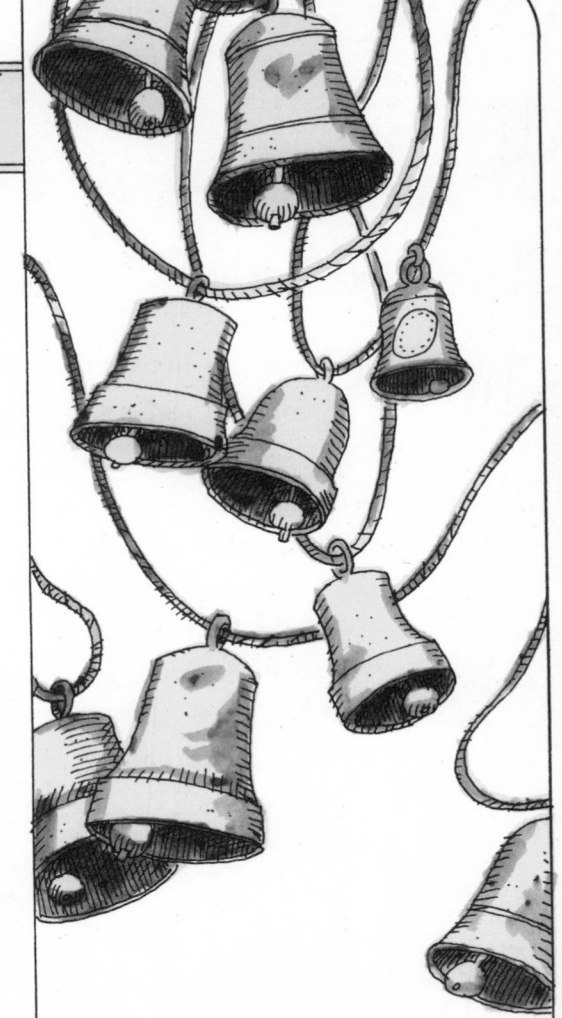

A bell that was big
   And gruff and bold
Bade good-bye
   To the year grown old.

A bell that was small
   And tinkled clear
Called greetings
   To the youngest year.

Then all the bells
   Joined the merry din
And the bright new year
   Was welcomed in.

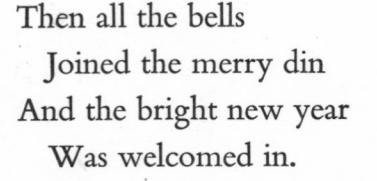

The Singing Bridge

We drove across a singing bridge,
  A singing bridge today.
A brook was tumbling
    underneath
  Along its rocky way.

I listened to the singing
    bridge,
  It hummed a special tune.
Over and over it sang to me,
  "Come back soon.
  "Come back soon."

ABOUT THE AUTHOR

Leland B. Jacobs' love for literature and his appreciation of its importance to children stems from his own childhood. Reared in a reading family, he began to write for pleasure when very young—and has continued to do so while pursuing a long and highly successful career as an educator. One of the foremost authorities in the field of children's literature, Dr. Jacobs is a professor of elementary education, specializing in language arts and children's literature at Teacher's College of Columbia University, and is widely known for his articles and lectures in this field.

ABOUT THE ARTIST

John E. Johnson is a free-lance illustrator who was raised in the heart of Pennsylvania Dutch country. Mr. Johnson, whose artwork has appeared widely on the pages of well known women's magazines, studied at the Philadelphia Museum School of Art. He is, at present, working on several books for children. A man whose favorite recreations are "eating and talking (not necessarily in that order)," Mr. Johnson, his wife (also an illustrator), and their two young children, live in New York City.